WORKBOOK PRESS LLC
187 E Warm Springs Rd
Suite B285 Las Vegas NV 89119 USA

Website: https://workbookpress.com/
Hotline: 1-888-818-4856
Email: admin@workbookpress.com

Ordering Information:

Quantity sales. Special discounts are available on quantity purchases by corporations, associations, and others. For details, contact the publisher at the address above.

ISBN-13:   978-1-963718-77-5 Paperback Version
              978-1-963718-78-2 Digital Version

REV. DATE: 07/19/2024

GUANAJA CHRONICLES
LAST RESORT

LANCE STARR

BOOK THREE

CHAPTER ONE

Setting: Rab Island, Croatia and Pacific Coast, Ecuador

Vanna didn't move, stiff. She could hear more than see. She could hear her heart beating and a normal breathing pattern. Now she could feel more than she could see. The weight on her midriff solid, unmoving to her senses. She shook her head now knowing, and the shake put her into dizziness again. She laid back waiting for it to pass; she realized she couldn't wait. She struggled around to get Lance's chest under her ear. World's alive, the breathing was equal to what she had listened for in the thousand hours he slept and she was awake, loving each inhale. She focused remembering a bleary dream of slow pulse and weak breath. It wasn't a dream and she hurried her ear up to his lips, his neck. No impediments, heartbeat pounding. The wave passed over her and she could do no more. Her head fell to his rippled chest.

She awoke again with all signs of his life continuing. She was lucid. He was sleeping, and shouldn't be. She called to him softly with no response. She panicked and increased the volume bouncing echoes in the cave, He blubbered, turned his head, and was gone again. Her military battle experience kicked in and she relaxed. A concussion may have provoked it, but at the moment he was deeply sleeping. She laid her head on his shoulder and dozed, not letting herself sleep.

All time-pieces on tanks or BCs were either smashed or consigned by the surf to the deep. She counted 1001, 1002, 1003, …. until she reached 1,500. Stiffness still hampering her, she moved her lips to his, re-confirming breath. She could feel the beating in his wrist. She loved this man, had to relinquish that, force a reaction, and a reawakening. Sometime earlier, who knows when he had had microseconds of clear eyes as he left gargling, Vanna tuned something about Guanaja, bombs, Yugoslavia. He faded as she fell prey to the devil bubbles.

Chipping a shard off her heart, she patted him on the cheek, calling his name. Nothing, a demanding slap, and volume. A shake of the head. She man-handled him around until she got his feet up-beach and his body raised over her breasts. She tried not to be hurtful but kept worrying his head keeping him awake. No counting now, a close observation she'd done for hours on end in the bowels of battleships. He began to fight back and confirmed hope. She cushioned his head firmly between his breasts and midriff. In this position, she could use a cross-chest carry to fight him off if it looked like he was going to get in front of her and give himself another concussion. She fought him and held tight until he went tired but awake.

"Lance, can you hear me, it's Vanna".

"Yes, I can hear you better than see you. Your voice is impacted deep in my heart. What are you doing here?"

"Lance, that's enough for the moment. Spend some time taking deep breaths. Remember, I am in my specialty area here. I know what I am doing. You WILL do what I say. Stay relaxed. I have done what I need to do for myself, now I need to get you ambulatory."

She reached over to his backpack and pulled out a white t-shirt. It was wet. She looked up and saw the missile silo-shaped cave vertical entrance. Water was dripping from the foliage on its edges. Better muddy or sweaty water than none at all. She wrung out the shirt, checked the taste, and squeezed it over his lips. He licked, trying to get as much water as his dry mouth cried out for.

"Lance, I'll get some more. Try to control your stress."

Vanna went sopping the shirt against the dripping green leaves. She squeezed it out removing some of the least tasty bits and sopped again. She returned with a full shirt and squeezed a more generous trickle to his lips and into his mouth. She wet the dry end of his tongue.

"Lance, stay still and wait again." She did ten more trips and gave herself three.

"Lance, roll to your left side. Don't try to rise. Go to your side, stop! Maintain consistent breathing. I'm counting the time."

"Now, ease to your back, similar breathing. Relax and move toward your right side. I will count again; this time, sit up slowly. If you don't feel dizzy, get to your feet; keep one hand on the wall to secure your balance. Stand with the support for a minute or two, then we'll walk normally."

"I'm up."

"Stop, do you feel dizzy or lack lucidity or feel nauseous?"

"I have a little residual headache; it's within my pain tolerance. What the hell are we doing here, and where is here?"

"Easy Lance, get your stress down. I'll tell you what I can, it isn't very much. If you look at that black water, you'll see it rides like a tide. A blast threw us at this, which turned out to be a cavern, or we'd be dead right now. I lost control of your head there, really sorry, you hit a granite wall. I got thrown around violently and temporarily went unconscious.

This was the first time I was able to fight back, get my head up, and protected on my midriff. I pulled some weed out of your esophagus and your breathing restarted after you threw up half the Adriatic. You gargled something about bombs. Fell out again and I lost the battle with my conscious. I don't know how long. I saw the missile silo shaped tunnel above us, rough edges, tried to cry out, failed. Or didn't hear anything. Let's sit down and reconnoiter. No rifle shot nor knife attack has taken you as close to death as this black tide. I'm sick that I couldn't keep your head in my arms away from the wall."

Lance rasped, "I'm clear headed now, less headache, and we need to see how we can get back to civilization. Don't spend energy being sorry for me; think about the other skills you applied and kept me alive. The obvious thing to start is calling up that tube. Let's alternate, I with bass tones and you with high soprano. All right, listen for a while to see if someone heard us. We don't know how far the silo extends."

Lance breathes, "That wasn't very successful. What else is obvious? I heard an echo that may or may not be real. What else, straight up.?"

Vanna hurries, "Lance, no! I spent half my time in base camp dealing with the physics of this kind of climbing. I see the problem clearly, maybe you haven't experienced it. If we try to walk up the wall with our backs and feet extended, the abrupt angles will shrug us off and we'll fall either to our death or injury that will stop us from exploring anything else. Let's follow the echo idea for now. Focus our faces toward what may be a back wall, alternate tones again, and look for anomalies. Use "hello" as the word now."

Several "hello's and another ten minutes gave no response. Lance followed up, "Vanna, I think I learned something. In the dark, it appears there is only one big wall back there. There were too many different responses of voice for only one reflecting surface. There must be another wall or another tunnel. Did either of our iPhones make it?"

Vanna rustles around, "they're both here. They were strapped inside the backpack. I have to go back to the overhead openings to see if they work. Ok, something is working, wait one! Dam, one speaker only crackles. The other is mashed. One mic is crushed. The other is "iffy". The light on one is fully charged. The other has maybe, half a charge. What do we do with that?"

"Vanna, there may be something we can do with light back there, look up. It will be dark in ten minutes, and I am bushed. I imagine you are. We've got to tuck in with the remains of the wet suits and sleep as much as we can tonight. Tomorrow, when the meager backup light reflects at the right angle, we can get further with iPhone lights."

"Vanna, this is the time; not the place, to hold you with thanks for another life."

"Accepted, easy on the holding of the bruised ribs."

CHAPTER TWO

Tunnel Dog

With tears in his eyes, Marko, on Zoom, told Roberto the horrid news. Roberto brushed off any blather about him owning a resort on the other side of the world. He honed in on the exact methods and times of searching. He gathered details of the Adriatic there and the shape and treachery of the shorelines and beaches. He googled "Rab" and printed out a topographic map of the island.

Roberto hurries, "Marko, get the police back to work with me. Two will be sufficient. Our friends have been lost completely for two days, correct. Get ropes and stretchers and first aid equipment including hydrating IV's. I will check Lance's itinerary on the computer here, try to duplicate, and call you from the plane with ETA for pick-up. No delay, with immediate transport to the shoreline. Marko, there are too many unknowns to give up and call this off in only two days. The tandem of Vanna and Lance are daringly impressive. Birdcage, out!"

Pedro Jet put them down on Roaban as the TACA jet was beginning to warm up. It took Roberto and partner a full eighteen hours with irritable delays in Miami and weather in Munich. He called Marko to the airport. The other passenger had a sleeping injection to make the trip tolerable. When they woke him, he was so woozy they couldn't fire right out searching. Roberto was lagged so Bucky licked him down until he slept for two hours. Roberto believed Bucky could be the key to this mystery. It took the police that long to arrive with the requested equipment.

HAPTER THREE

Day Three, Dripping Water And Rubbing Plants

As typical, Vanna caught the glimmer first. Not so typical, she immediately shook Lance back to the living. She checked and updated his symptoms. The headache was only a reminder occasionally. He was hungry and all the foodstuffs in the backpack had washed away. Vanna, with a leaf bridge, rewired the dripping water from the walls for immediate hydration. Now, an unpleasant reminder of "Seal Time." She searched among the plants and leaves on the silo walls bringing two handfuls of green edibles that really could have been improved with salt. Lance, who might have been tempted to grouse, didn't. She went back for a second handful of each. Deep draughts of now cleaner water, badly needed, filled them up.

Lance quickly exhaled. They needed to search before they lost the meager sunlight. They retrieved the iPhone. They went gingerly without batteries until they hit what darkness was a wall. It dissipated into black as they clung to the left. A short distance to the right, the lapping of water again could be heard. Reaching to the left, the wall ended; the lapping was closer below us. It hadn't ended but broke off to the left appearing in our dim light to form the edge of a huge box or some kind of ragged terrain. There was no catwalk or ridge. The only way to go further could be suicide.

The depth of water was too deep to register on any of our tree limbs dunked to check. There could be currents carrying us out to sea or back into never-ending darkness. No idea of implements or rocks or blockages.

Lance, trying to speak to get an echo got very little, one double repeat back where they had met the water. "The echo wasn't much.

I did see a second wall beyond this one. No sign of shadow or anything. Rushing water to the right. Returning and looking for another track is our only option.

They moved more quickly back the path they had forged to no success. When they started to see slight shadows, they were at the point in the wall where they had turned left. Lance cranked up the fully charged iPhone and showed it ahead. Solid wall, indeed, it went off into a "Y" variation competing two ways into the distance. One was parallel to our first old friendly wall. Lance moved immediately with light into the wall angle veering to the left. He returned after five minutes with the light extinguished.

Vanna, "Well, did you see something?"

"Lance, the general answer is "no."

"Is there some other specific answer?"

"Let me think for a minute." The forty seconds he pondered about drove Vanna wild.

"So?"

"Here's what I can say. The walkway is smooth, and regular, with no holes nor jagged edges as far as I went. There were no crossed paths on any side. A single walkway. There were no other things that I judged helpful except for two unevenly gouged tracks up four feet on the right wall. There was only water below them. There is no light. I saw these scratches only with my phone; we'll have to go above them."

"Lance, any thoughts?"

"Vanna, you have been a better planner than me for years. I can only suggest some probabilities, I wish I could be certain of something. I'll start and you stop me when I miss something or anything. Our choices include venturing into the black surf and being saved or worse swept out to sea. Currents could take us beyond search parameters or against ragged shores and final concussions. We have 'O' hints of what might be there."

"We could foolishly try to climb the silo which you have convinced me would be suicide. Trying to yell up some communication has gained nothing. This "Y" shaped wall is a major risk, and dangerous. The danger is at least obvious to us. Echoes have hinted little. Those only led to that last path leading us into unknown water. Over, under, around, and through, this "Y" path is the only thing that doesn't already predict our doom."

"I agree. I see nothing else. We need to go back and get our backpacks with whatever tools may remain in them, wetsuits for sleeping, and any rehydration inventions."

They gathered what they could avoided using their phones as much as possible, and carefully felt their way into the unknown.

CHAPTER FOUR

Cainine Leads

Bucky was first to recover. With a wash of his damp tongue on his cheek, Roberto leaped to his feet. The two policemen, monitoring everything, smiled and got to their feet. Roberto shook Marko and sent him to Anika to locate any clothes Vanna or Lance had worn. Roberto called Bucky over. Bucky stopped, smelled, and headed flying to the surf on the north end of the beach. He stopped, smelled, and whined. That was accurate because that is where Vanna and Lance had headed in and down to the wedding.

Roberto took Bucky up onto one of the craggy rock formations blocking the sea from the shore. He repeated the smell reminder to no attention from Bucky. Bucky ran in every direction navigable for three hours before he put his head down to rest.

Roberto had studied all the winds, currents, and caves already known and searched. He now looked for any evidence of explosives. He looked around the terrain and took the clothes and Bucky further from the shore. He let him free and he scampered for another two hours. It was sundown on what would be the fourth day. Roberto could not release Bucky and give up for today. He fed him and he voluntarily drank a lot of water.

Roberto didn't have to give anything to smell. He guided Bucky to scour in parallel lines to the increasing altitudes from the shore. Roberto hadn't learned only about motivating shrimp in his Marine Science Masters. With maps in Guanaja, he was on the ground running when he saw similar landforms here. He also knew the ugly realities of time lost in oceanic environments. They continued into the night. Bucky always was the favorite of Lance, and knew who he was smelling for. He would search for two hours and eat and drink and rest for one-half.

CHAPTER FIVE

Almost Passed In The Night

The two lost lovers hurried in the dark for two hours without stopping. They carefully helped each other over the four feet raised blocks returning down to the original level. All continued to be dark. There were odd scrapings on the walls. They rested for fifteen minutes and dragged themselves to their feet. Another hour and they had to hydrate and rest, not sleep. Forty-five minutes later, they began to sense twilight. Adrenaline hit the arteries and they sped up. Fifteen minutes later, they came to another full wall stopping them in their tracks. Losing their drive, they collapsed and scoured the area. It was light, at least, and finally, they spotted the source.

Looking more closely, they again felt disappointment. It was a rusted metal door pounded into the bedrock. Around the edges, light was sleeping in. Searching around the edges, they could see a continuation of a walkway and wall for the fifteen feet they could see.

After a half hour of resting, hydrating, and wishing there were some disgusting plants to eat, Lance stirred and said, "The only way out of here is not back. We've got to get through this door as small as its opening is. You'll fit fine. I better practice holding my breath."

Vanna answers, "We don't have the door open."

"Ok, I'm not going to make any headway with my knuckles. What tools survived the deluge, something in a backpack?"

"Wait one!" Vanna continues, "There's something; not much.

A climbing chisel may be some help. I guess you may have had some plan to climb somewhere.

"I don't remember."

Tiredly, Vanna adds, "There are the two cutting torches. One tank is definitely broken and empty. I'm not sure about the other. Try the chisel first."

Lance jimmied the chisel blade into the thin opening between the metal and wall. Nothing. He tried the three other openings and got an inch and a half with one. He sat to rest. Vanna's brute strength in many areas is unbelievable, but not here.

"Vanna, I'm weakening. On the other hand, I don't want to live another day without some success. I'll keep at this, and look for a weakness. See if you can do something with that torch."

Vanna de-connected, re-hooked, bled gas to see if there was some, and finally returned to Lance.

"Lance, I may have some moderately good news. I'm far from sure. Any more gain with the chisel?"

"Yeah, I got it open enough to put your foot through. I need a break. Let's see what happens with the torch. It's small. Backpack sized."

"They fired up the torch, not a blast. He went back to the spot where he had foot room for Vanna and cut at the hinge. It broke and the door bent, crunching, back enough to get two shoes through. He went to the adjacent hinge, cut it in half, and the torch went out. He tried it over and over. The gas was depleted."

He crawled over to Vanna, equally disappointed, and rested his cheek on her thigh. "Honey, I'm not giving up. I have no spirit to do anything now. I need to rest. I'll get up in the night and continue. I don't need the light for the chisel."

CHAPTER SIX

Man, And Dog Rappel

Roberto dozed and watched Bucky following parallel furrows, feeling guilty that he couldn't do more. It was beginning to lighten in the east over the nearest highlands. He got up to give what he expected would be the final feeding of the morning when Bucky began running in circles, first, then barking and whining. Marko and the police were asleep, and Roberto scaled the furrows like a needy goat. Stopping for a minute to orientate himself, he could see the surf off the breakwater in the distance and a huge hole at his feet. Two more steps and he would be the lost one. Bucky could knock him off the edge in excitement and sharp barks. With Bucky like this, there was no doubt in his mind.

Roberto yelled loud enough to wake the quick and the dead and the police. Marko stirred hopefully, the only bilingual person here, he struggled to his post-grad legs. He had drunk enough beers with Roberto, he knew well when to get serious. In the distance, squinting, he heard Roberto call for the searchlight, power battery, rope, and firehouse wooden ladders. He translated that to the police and they responded correctly. He tore hard to Roberto.

The situation was obvious. Roberto snarled, "Marko, do you know anything about this big hole? Did the searchers miss it, did you, do you know how deep it is, what it is?"

"Roberto, I played in most of these areas when I was a kid. I would surely have seen it. This has to be something drilled here sometime during the Croatian Separation War. If it's deep, we may find the explosive that started this nightmare."

Roberto taken aback, "Didn't the explosion go out into the Adriatic?"

"I think so but don't know. I just don't know. Paula jumped into me and I didn't register until I felt her and her obvious wounds. My focus was nowhere else. According to others injured, it would have been coming out of the North. Unless there was another blast, which I would have noted, it went quickly from the right of the beach spreading wildly in a whirlpool of damaging pressure. From the right, not the left. Not here from the left side. It was coming in this direction."

"Marko, I want you to get these guys aiming the searchlight down there right now. We're not waiting till daylight. If they will give a bit of twilight, we're going. Put out the ropes for rappelling. I'll buckle Bucky up in a harness. Let him down in tandem with me so if he hits a crag or other danger, I can steer him."

Bucky whined a little when he was lifted over the edge, quieted, and rolled up into a fetal position. Roberto kept a hand on him as often as possible. He watched for anything that might be an explosive; and met the wet floor without problem.

Bucky howled, barked and snorted to get his harness off. He went in circles smelling every corner and abandoned backpack. Roberto took him back to a leash, too dangerous to let him run into the black unknown. He soon lurched over to the wall tugging Roberto the forty yards. Roberto's small flashlight was enough to deduce from walls, angles, and tracks the probable path for the trapped runners. Bucky knew exactly where they ran.

With his small light, Roberto had seen plenty. Bucky only confirmed it. He dragged the fighting dog back to the opening to communicate above.

"Marko, we need more. The pattern of the blast here is not accidental even though it may not be the cause of the beach carnage. I don't see or smell anything. I think we need to buck up our defense while we run with the hunt. We need another man.

We need to select cautiously. I can't have some Yugoslavian cop with war anger still simmering purposely denying knowledge of this silo. I can't have you because I need you to translate up there. You were here during the war and communicated your danger to me on Zoom. Have an "informal" talk with these guys and steer me away from more trouble."

CHAPTER SEVEN

Reluctant National Police Support

Hurriedly, Marko separated the men and spoke quietly one at a time. The one guy wouldn't say a thing. The other guy, very cautiously, told him that the first guy had lost family in the fighting. From what that guy could find out, my family couldn't determine that my kin weren't involved. It was 90% confirmed that another tribe had been guilty. Firmly ordered by his lieutenant officers to bury the past, repressing the doubt, they had been backing each other up appropriately in their police roles.

Marko walked away. He returned to the communication, speaker-off with Roberto in the silo. He told Roberto what had been said.

"Marko, you're going to have to trust your instincts. Think about their hand gestures, voice tension, eye movement, nervousness, hesitations, or other things you might identify."

"Roberto, we need to move. I'm going to rule out the first guy that wouldn't talk to me. They could both be innocent bystanders. I don't have time to pry it out of the police department because they were chosen. I'll keep watching for anything dangerous and either contact you or act myself if you are in danger."

"Ok, send #2 down; we need more rope. Put the searchlight on its rollers, ease it down making sure the battery is full. Have a medium size cutting torch and tank standing by. Somehow pack the guy with a dozen or more liter bottles of water. Call Anika to send up some canned meat and three loaves of bread. Send three packs of blankets, and get four revolvers from Anika whose late husband had several. If she has silencers, get those. Keep those out of sight in the packing. You do the packing. Marko, you keep one of those pistols. You don't need a silencer up there. If you have dog food, send a couple of cans. Bucky is too excited to eat. Don't leave your protective position. Have Anika or one of the scuba trainers bring the stuff. Send the light now, and hold on to the cutting torch. I have to get back there ASAP for whatever waits. Bucky indicates life. If I have any antenna access, I will contact you to send it. Granite cliffs may interrupt the signal. If not, listen for a click, or after an hour, send it even without my signal. I need the carbon arc light and battery now. If you send anything without my signal, you'll have to send the other cop with it, or better, if the scuba trainer is there, send him."

I had to fight Bucky tooth and nail until the searchlight arrived. He didn't need any light. There was water in the structure. Splashing him with some, I relented and headed out.

CHAPTER EIGHT

Mobility Around A Rusty Door

Lance woke up at midnight and hammered and twisted on the impacted rectangle of rust.

"Sleep, Vanna. I'm afraid tomorrow will bring more stress. I'll sleep when I can't stand."

He finally slept before the glimmer began to glow in the walled corners. The momentum he had gained showed more long hours ahead. Vanna saw him collapse and rose to see what the glimmer would expose. Drawing from deep inside, keeping her noise down, she lay on her back to see what parts of her might slip through. She could get her legs to her hips up against the panel. She stepped back and found the chisel, silver now from the scraping rust. She sat and used the chisel not to hammer, but to bend and bend again the panel to move it away from the impacted wall. She shifted her focus away from the granite hitting the metal on the rebound. She was afraid she would wake Lance, but couldn't sit here stymied when her angle of view began to show more room for hips. She would have to free his bigger hips and six-pack if she got to the other side, hips scraped or not.

CHAPTER NINE

Stuck, Forever?

Stumbling, keeping his balance against the wall, Roberto kept Bucky in sight as he tried to leap ahead. There was no sense of death in Bucky's gate nor responses. The opposite. He would sense better than humans what to expect in the black distance. Horses evinced that same sense. The path jutted left unexpectedly. Roberto fell against the wall, grabbing granite and scraping it in the palm of his hands.

Swearing, standing again, he hoped he was correctly reading Bucky's actions. Sooner than he had wished, he rammed the handle on the searchlight. The iPhone may be needed later. He forced Bucky to heel, and quickly as the floor' sloped up, moved forward in bright arc-lit passages. Another lunge from Bucky confirmed without a doubt, the right passage. The intense burn from the arc washed out any glow that might be reflected in the distance.

CHAPTER TEN

Seriously Stuck, De-Hydrated

Vanna had struggled, this time with noticeable success. She would wake Lance in enthusiasm and show him how cleverly she got through. She pushed her shoes grinding into the wall of metal, pushed them again further into the middle opening, again into the opening of an exit on the opposite side. She tolerated the scratches on her hips as she forced them over the rough floor toward the other exit. She manhandled her shoulders toward the exit, shrugged them, and growled in pain. She threw them backward and forward now scratching her breasts to bleeding. She halted and uttered the Seals most distinguished profanity repeatedly. Her shoulders were too wide to go through. Her hips had flowed painfully around the edges. There was no way she could strain her tendons, in agony, to thrust her shoulders through. She had to stop; the pain was too great. She was sure Lance would make fun of her; she HAD to CRY OUT.

That was not SOP for a Seal. Lance came flying against the granite until, in trauma, he saw the blood and heard the pain. He knew she was horrified to sound off so hard. He could never get more than his hands close to her.

"Vanna, are you holding your back up to avoid bleeding, or is that position ok for you for a while."

"Lance, I'm so sorry. I should have had you with me. I'm ashamed, my shoulder and back are searing beyond my tolerance. My breasts are stinging and bleeding. I don't know, Oh."

"Vanna, hold your back up for a minute more. I'll get you."

Lance ran over in the dim glow, located the backpacks, and pulled out all the wetsuit material still usable. He ran back again, put his head and the one hand he could force in. With the wetsuit in it, raised her shoulder as high as it would stretch and folded the three-quarter-inch rubber suit into a four-ply pillow. He waited until she eased her way back into it, and heard her limited relief.

Vanna huffed, "There's more trouble here."

Lance, close to tears, said, "I see it. It will be much more difficult; I will solve it somehow. Can you move back this way, or sideways in any direction?"

Vanna, "Let me check." A painful pause. "Ok, I can wriggle back to the point where the width of my hips grinds into the rusted metal. My arms are free."

"Vanna, here's our first move. I'm crying for the pain this may cause. I'll put my arm back in again, put my palm under the makeshift pillow, and raise you again. Not stretching you up as much as I did before, should leave an open space for you to move your hips left and right carefully. Move it only until the scratches react, then come back the same. Stop anytime you need to. I will have no trouble supporting you while you get a breath. You will have to do this until you get your hips, thighs, and legs facing me. The shoulders will have to wait. First, wiggle and press your hips until they slip out into the opening between the walls."

What you need to do now may fail; we must try. Get your hips on my side of you, that is, your hips and legs pointing in my direction from you're wrenched wall space. Here's the rub: you need to roll over to your back and slide the wet suit under to soothe. Swing your hips until you can straighten your legs out toward me, toward the entrance you first used. Roll face-up again.

"Vanna, I am making a pillow of my cleaner shirt. When I can reach your head close to the metal here, raise and put the wet suit under your thighs to protect them while I put the pillow back under your head.

CHAPTER ELEVEN

What The Hell?

"Lance, can you give me five to try to straighten out wrinkled skin pinched around the suit and shirt?"

"I may need more than that to invent a method to get your shoulders back on this side and into less pain."

Lance turned back to ruffle through the backpacks when a brilliant glare, shocking eyes dilated in the dark, knocked him to his knees.

"What the hell?" he saw nothing in the glare.

A shadow stepped out beside the light, ghostly in form, moving quickly toward him, saying "And Dios Mio to you too", pulling him up and hugging him.

"Roberto?"

"Roberto, and Bucky."

Bucky gave him the full bath.

"This police guy came to do any heavy lifting. He's armed."

"What the hell are you doing here, where I don't even know where is?

"Lance, where's Vanna?"

"She's back here, stuck, and we need help. She tried to do the Seal 'tough rush', alone and her shoulders are too wide."

Roberto now in shock, "why, how?"

"Roberto, we can't explain now. Both of us need medical care and I don't know how to get out or where we'll be if we get out."

"But I just rappelled down that missile silo and Bucky found you."

Vanna croaked, "Roberto, no!"

Roberto started, astonished.

Lance quickly followed, "Roberto, Vanna has analyzed that egress and projects one dead and others injured to the point they can't be evacuated. She has some serious Seal experience and I agree with her. We have tried every black wall and corner. You may have seen the surf in the cave when you came down. That's where we were thrown in here with concussions. Although now she knows she shouldn't have tried it alone, Vanna is going the way we'll have to go."

Roberto assesses, "Let me look at Vanna and this metal frame you're describing. Stay still, I won't hurt you, Vanna, dulce."

"Well, Lance, you and Vanna are the main planners usually. I can see in your eye dilation that all is not well. I'll take a crack at it, as you gringos call it. I have blankets, more water and food for us and Bucky up above. There also should be a cutting torch arriving. We're getting some silenced pistols which Marko will hide in the blankets. This guy doesn't speak English so let's keep it down. The last war here was not long enough ago to now know who loves whom. Any bomb, while maybe not be related to the past, can't be ignored."

Lance adds, "Well, communication could be difficult, too. I did tell Marko, your old roommate, to lower these things down if

I didn't call or ping somehow sooner. What have you got on your cell phone?"

"Everything! Don't forget I'm still in a running battle with the Cartel. The granite foundation here may be a problem. GPS may be a bit stronger. Does Marko have GPS?"

Vanna answers, "I believe he does; would you use my regular phone and try to raise him? If you can, get a click-through; he'll get busy. I need to close my eyes for a moment."

Vanna lay back and Roberto ruminated his next move. He turned off the phone but got no reception. He walked to all corners and back down the path: nothing strong enough for a sickly click. Vanna raised again, trying to avoid going to sleep. They had smiles for each other and she realized what he was doing.

The cop had sat down dozing against the wall near the searchlight.

"No luck, Roberto, she murmured?"

"Zip"

"I've been lying here staring up thinking there is some tiny spot above. I'm not to be moving much. I may be hallucinating. Before you brought the searchlight, I thought that spot might be where some of the glimmer comes from. Give me your phone and I'll see if my jail here isn't below some weaker or thinner layer of granite. She raised herself to take the phone."

"Marko, Marko, Vanna calling, come in, over"

There was no slight noise indicating anything.

Vanna, unsure said, "Let me move my shoulders back to the portal which I hope will be our exit." Roberto sat and waited.

She called again, no response for some time. Seconds crawled like hours.

She called again and as if no one had been home, she got static. She waited again and got extended static. Fogged mind, she considered the alternatives. Did he hear her on a normal connection and couldn't respond? Was he able to understand her? Were the batteries too depleted? She wouldn't accept any hopelessness.

She adjusted her phone, Roberto's, and called, "Marko, Marko, this is Vanna. Add GPS to your calling app. respond, over". She got a firm click and a crackled "Marko". Then nothing. She heard static that every iPhone user would understand, the machine was being adjusted, or re-positioned.

A horrid feedback, Marko's hurried voice. "I've got you, Vanna, for now. Know I've already sent the torch and others. If I lose you...... signal back to GPS."

Lance, "She woke him up. Lance, I got Marko for three seconds on Roberto's phone. The granite above me in this case is thinner. He said some things were on the way with the other diver. I lost him and can't reconnect."

"Roberto?"

"I'm here Lance, I'm coming. I'm leaving the phone with Vanna."

"Roberto, listen if I conk out again. There is a gas-cutting torch coming. Other food and supplies. You or the diver need to unpack. There are three pistols in there. I want you to take one, conceal it, and give one to Vanna and me, also concealed. You can trust the diver with any of this, not the cop until we confirm his true colors. Marko was leery but only had the two to pick from before the diver arrived. Shine the light back down the entrance pathway to help them find us. It'll be a few minutes; I need to rest again."

Vanna, in the distance, "I heard that. Roberto, minimize his sleeping. Short intervals only."

CHAPTER TWELVE

Fraud Flags Presented And Snuffed

Huffing noises in the distance. Search-light refocused. Vanna, still trapped; moving to an angle that might reduce her pain. Cop stood up against the wall. Lance and Robert, shoulder to shoulder as they had so often been, moved back to shield the reflections. The cop heard a voice in the distance and stood, freezing in place. Vanna, relieved, looked over at the cop as the diver stepped into the light. The cop pulled his gun. Vanna screamed; Roberto's burly fist hammered the pistol to the floor. No delay, he had been on guard since the inception. The cop dived to retrieve it. The diver hammered his foot into the cop's hand, putting his other foot on his neck cutting off any vision.

Roberto, realizing he'd been late in getting these down here, stepped quickly to the bundled blanket pulling and handing a pistol to Lance, reached another to Vanna, checked the load of a third, and kept it in his hand.

Lance quickly to the diver, "Berndt, I'll get some ropes or rather, Berndt do you have any metal wire in there?"

Responding and moving the foot off the hand, "There's some bonding the gas tank to the torch, if not somewhere else. I'll get it."

Lance charges, "No, Berndt, Roberto, get it. Keep your foot on that hand until we can search him."

They kept him down and found a lead slug, a knife, and a stun grenade. Tied up with wire, they stood him up to see three silenced pistols aimed at his head, Vanna on her elbow. Ornery, slapped himself back to the wall.

Taking a breath, they looked at each other. Berndt now saw the cop in the light and froze, anger and disgust on his face.

Berndt snarls, "Lance, this guy is sick with things that happened in the last war. How he got to be a cop beats me. I need to talk to him, and it will have to be in Croatian. If we ever get out of here, I will inform you. In the meantime, while we are mounting this escape, you need to cede all responsibility for him, all, to me: life or death."

{Translation: Berber, and don't doubt that a lot of people know you, you need to listen to me right now. If you refuse to listen and take heed, you will be back in jail or worse. A traitor cop will have a nightmare in jail time.}

You are carrying human anger for people you knew who were killed or injured. There are lots of others who have lost, and hurt, but remain "Humane." I lost my brother, my closest friend and idol. I feel pain every day. You can and must repress this, struggle against that emptiness, and live a decent life. I have that pain, but have a diving job, a decent salary and benefits package, and can live a tolerable life. You are working with a partner who was on the other side. As an Emergency Sea Officer, I see your reports and professional activities. You have been able to tolerate him and give appropriate back-up when required. That is exactly what you are required to do. If friendship should develop, that would be a bonus. Your actions here may or may not cause a suspension or other punishment. That is not my decision to make. My decision here is to get these people to safety. You have three ways this can go:

1. Behave and support and hope for clemency since you didn't kill or hurt someone.

2. Try to escape and find my foot again on your neck deciding where to drive in the heel causing permanent disability.

3. Kill you on the spot if your actions endanger any of these people or me. (End translation.)

CHAPTER THIRTEEN

The Right Technology Or We're Dead

Trendt came back to English and we ascertained that Berber was incapacitated against damaging us or our plans.

Roberto entered the conversation, "If these bars are not titanium or worse, this torch should work slowly and accurately. Vanna, here are some dinner choices and a blanket. No candles; all but one of us will be joining you. One of us will always be with you. We'll start this cutting in the morning. At that point, you will need to move your limbs as far as possible from the cutting points. You can cover yourself with a blanket."

"Before you sleep, I assume Lance will apply all the antibiotics and dressings. We brought everything along in the pistol blankets. Getting Marko into a signal access cell location will be the most critical event of our rescue."

Vanna, in the least comfortable body position, kept an eye on Berber in the night. Turning the arc light on in what his watch said morning, Roberto woke her. Lance was dozing into twilight and the cop would be weak from his lack of sleep-in wires, as was the plan.

"Vanna, move over in the corner as much away from me as possible. Keep your blanket away from the flames; shade your eyes. Try to get some sign from Marko above. Use GPS however it works. If you have to use Morse code, we'll hope he knows it."

Lance sat up and turned away as Roberto lit off the gas cutter. That stirred the cop who also was smart enough to turn away. The bars were not titanium, but steel that reacted to the welding gas. It went slow. Everyone was praying the gas would not run out before the cutting was done. A larger opening was needed in front of Roberto; then he had to enter the cell and cut a similar shoulder-wide hole in the opposite side. Vanna stayed inside the cell. That was the only place they had raised Marko the night before. She kept the blanket up and her head away.

Lance prepared all the food and tools to be divided between backpacks. He loaded himself and the hunky diver with the most Despite the fact they had to maneuver the arc light into the dark of the other side. Forever, was 45 minutes, and Roberto finished openings on both sides. Now he had to guide the cutter ahead in case of other metal obstructions. Vanna brought the blanket and called repeatedly to Marko.

Marko undoubtedly had been sleeping. Her constant noise prodding brought a squawk. She took a shot at questioning "Morse". No response for minutes to hours of the length of ten minutes. In Morse, 'diver knows'. The other driver had raced from the dock across the island with other supplies, not usable now, maybe later.

Lance recommends, "Vanna, go ahead, your Morse is better than mine and you know what and where as well as any of us."

"Got it. Get everybody and everything through the holes. Roberto, do you have a compass?"

"Sorry, my cell is for eluding cartel animals."

CHAPTER FOURTEEN

Deadly Cliffside

Vanna urges, "All right, we'll use Seal 'dead reckoning. Comments are welcome. Let me bring you into my thinking. We walked from the surf west to the double wall where we turned north. We didn't change direction noticeably and ran into this elbow. West again now through the bars. Everybody minimizes cell use and moves west. I will code, "Moving, watch west".

The cop was dragging the speed down until Trendt took him by the neck. The eyes bulged and he sped up.

Vanna, Morse code, "West see, use GPS. Moving as fast as we can will make it more noticeable to them."

The layer of rock was thinning. No voice was heard either way. The path turned into a harrowing walkway next to a 30-foot fall into ragged granite.

The searchlight was critical and unwieldy. Lance joined Trendt in jockeying it around what became a 50-yard breathless traipse. Roberto handled the torch and tank himself. Vanna kept a hand against the wall, stopping to try the connection again and again.

It was forty yards past the tightrope before a crackle. Everyone including the cop was running with sweat. Vanna sent another cryptic burst. This time a complete sentence returned. "Burdan here, are you receiving? Lance turned to Trendt, "Yes that's our other diver. Vanna, try voice."

"This is Vanna. Do you need Morse code or do you hear me?" A crackle everyone could hear growled through, Burdan said four words, and the burst took him out again. Vanna impatiently paused, and quickly asked, "Are we on GPS?" Response, "GPS yes, voice intermittent."

Vanna again, "Are we heading west?"

Burdan crackles, "I only heard 'heading', assume direction, yes west."

Vanna to Lance, "Anything else you want, anybody."

Trendt responded, circling the light. "Look, thirty meters ahead, I see an opening, only darkness within.

Vanna back, "Burdan, proceeding west, can you confirm you are right above us?"

Burdan, "According to GPS, within a radius of 7 meters."

CHAPTER SIXTEEN

Follow The Dog

Bucky had stopped arguing the path when they finally went where he whined. When they got to the elbow, he watched every move the cop made. He was comfortable only with Lance, Vanna, and Roberto. Trendt didn't get any welcome. A completely unknown human.

When Roberto slammed the Berber's pistol, Bucky spurted to Lance's side with a glance toward Vanna. He easily vaulted the holes in the metal trap Roberto had opened and took the lead which he first smelled and trotted west.

The thirty meters melted away and at the option, Bucky smelled both north and West on the trails. He moved to lead West, and everybody stopped. He growled, yellow-orange eyes in the arc light. They just stood there.

Vanna, "Burdan, have you recovered our trail?"

"Still within seven yards."

"Burdan, we've come to a branch tunnel. Look at elevations; should we continue West or turn north? The dog is whining to go west."

Burdan, "I'm not knowledgeable of this area nor is anybody else. North of here either stays level or goes further into the mountain. Elevation as a guide, I'd follow the dog."

On into the arc-lighted path, orange eyes flickering and returning. If we didn't know exactly who was blinking those eyes, we'd feel like we were in a monster movie. We passed other three-quarters of a mile in darkness. Bucky howled, returning to try to egg us on. He saw it before we did, of course, and some soft dim rays soon surrounded us.

Breathless, Roberto gasped, "I hope we aren't approaching another missile silo."

Lance answered, turning the arc down, "Chances are Bucky has already been down there. We have no dog/human language for that."

Vanna sped to contact. "Burdan, do you still have us. Do you see a wash-out in the hill, if it is a hill?"

Burdan, "Vanna, we are still within 7 meters of you. There is some kind of landform, not exactly a hill, a rise coming toward us. Our communication has cleared. Either the ground layer is thinner here or we've lost the granite. Hang on!"

The dependability of communication raised spirits. All but one.

"Burdan, this is Trendt. You've got to order a bus immediately. We've got an attempted murder the court will have to sort out. Don't share this near the other cop if he is there. If so, keep an eye on him."

"Will do, hang on."

Marko called out excitedly, "Bucky's here. Burdan, tell Vanna he's here. Come on, follow him."

They ran the last thirty yards. Bucky was running circles around the lip of a rock. It was narrow, and thin, the shape of an open snake's mouth, or maybe a salamander. You could imagine a slimy pointed tongue flipping out of it. Bucky kept barking leery of going in there again.

Marko got down and tried to slide to whatever cavern was below. He had a knapsack on and couldn't wiggle through. His loosened small rocks and gravel; got an "S O B" from below. Trendt. He hurried back to Burdan and asked him to inform Vanna.

Roberto said, "I'll take this, Lance, you still have eyes that beg rest. Marko, we're sending Vanna up to see if she fits. Be there for her."

Vanna dumped her blanket and gave the radio and a kiss to Lance. She tightened her clothes wishing she had some Vaseline or sun cream to make a smoother glide for her chest. It took her ten painful minutes to get to where Marko could pull her gently out.

She called back down, "Gentlemen, there is a chance. If you can't squeeze tight enough, we'll have to get a CAT to open the hole. There is no way you can get the arc light or torch equipment out."

Roberto replies. "I'm not gonna stay in here until a CAT comes from who knows where no matter what width of skin I wear off. Marko, please."

"Right here, Roberto."

"Do you have the pistol?"

"Yes."

"Check that it is loaded and functioning. We're sending Berber up next. His ankles will remain wired; he will need to use his arms. Don't wait a minute to re-wire his wrists even while he is being pulled out the last few feet. Trendt will be up next to take him into custody. Trendt, I think you'll have to go immediately behind to push him up until Marko can get a hold of him. Watch out for his feet."

It took fifteen minutes of grueling wrestling with rocks and dirt to get the two up. Trendt slipped out as the "bus" arrived, rounded up the other cop, and along with two other armed officers on the bus escorted Berber to be booked.

Time for the last two. Roberto firmly decided he would go last, joking not to act like a captain of a ship, but because Lance with his big lungs and rippling back muscles would open more clearance for him to get through.

CHAPTER SEVENTEEN

Hospital Dog Under The Bed

On top of their concussions, Vanna and Lance had lost skin. Anika loaded them up with hydrates and lost no time to the hospital. Lance commanded Bucky to go with Marko. Whining he complied.

The emergency room staff lofted them quickly onto rolling beds, looking into eyes and starting saline hydration.

The injured duo had to stay in the hospital for two weeks of tests and strict bed rest. Still feeling guilty for their pain, Marko stopped in intermittently to visit. Roberto didn't leave their side; slept in a cot from war years. Bucky, back at camp was inconsolable. People had trouble sleeping over his whining. Finally, when Lance could sit up enough to look out the window, they brought Bucky over to be waved at. That helped.

Marko brought Bucky over when he was picking Petra up to take her home. Fast as a slash of lightning, Marko embracing Petra, Bucky jumped up the fire steps and sliding unerringly under Lance's bed, with Vanna laughing on. It took some serious coaxing to get him out of the hospital and home. At that point, he sensed they were alright. They were released three days later. Upon arrival, they got a full tongue washing on every point of skin Bucky could access.

CHAPTER EIGHTEEN

Will It Be Parasailing?

The hospital had been very conservative, watching them carefully till the day they were released. They were told they could dive only to one atmosphere for two weeks. After that one week limited to 45 feet thereafter returning to regular depths. No lifting of tanks out of the water until after four weeks.

Two days after return, Vanna started her inescapable seduction. Lance said, I'm not ready. I'm afraid I'll hurt you.

Lay beside me. I'm not injured more than you, and I'm fine. You know how to caress me with no weight. Hope you didn't forget. Devil in her eyes. He slipped to 45 degrees from her body. It came unusually slow, then a final huge wrestle of her upper body put the proof to it. It had been well past enough. The bungalow slats vibrated with her joy.

The next night, "If you're still worried about the scratches on my breasts, which are only pink traces, get over and behind me. The following morning, all concerns had been addressed."

CHAPTER NINETEEN

Ecuadoric Parasailing?

In their breathless bubbles after love, they had been discussing Lance's long-time dream of Ecuador and parasailing. After two weeks day and night with little to do in the hospital, they had formulated some plans. Many articles were out showing expats from several countries retiring there. If they were Americans, they could get bonfire residence and remain exempt from funding the dregs of Trumpian once-allied government-bashing.

They discussed their plans with Anika and the guys still manning a lot of the wreck diving. They had plans for opening a parasailing club off Guayaquil and settling, or if not, setting up a joint operation with the guys a kilometer or more up into a protected outcropping of Croatia, Rab. Complicated financial auditioning provided fair division pending what was decided. A secondary backup plan offered a closer jointly shared parasailing operation sharing client's coupons between resorts according to the use of scuba and parachutes.

CHAPTER TWENTY

Not Only The Climate Is Hot In Guayaquil

They planned a visit to Cuenca, the expat place, as well as Guayaquil, a possible new parasailing option for tourists. There were only three along the whole coast. There were surprisingly small scuba operations. Usually, those two sports are related in tandem. Maybe there was a market.

With medical capabilities becoming more important in their lives, they were given intense tours of three hospitals and senior living facilities. They met with many people older than them and a few younger. Some had had careers around seas and oceans.

They settled into a moderate size hotel for the Guayaquil visit. They wanted to see the life they might join there, see if there were any hidden, uncomfortable surprises. The food was delicious in the hotel, right on the ocean for seafood. They wandered further afar and after dinner stopped at a bar with a sea view, moon and all. There had been some Germans in the woodpile because the beer was excellent. There was a lot of activity and jostling as the evening drew on. We moved on towards our hotel to another street full of people passing, dancing; jostling by. In the hotel, we stopped at the bar to have an aquavit and sweet dreams. As most bars plan, there was no clock in the bar. Lance looked at his watch for the time, and it wasn't there. Sickness hit the pit of his stomach. He had been pickpocketed. Where, he had no idea. He hurried to talk to the bar tender whose English was out of a drinks menu. He was directed to the night manager who was fluent.

The story has been told a thousand times. There was nothing the hotel could do. You could try the police. You were in the crowd out there. The only slim glimmer of hope was going to the thieves market tomorrow and seeing if it was there. You could buy it back. Lance tossed and grumbled all night.

He slugged his breakfast down and we headed via taxi, who knew exactly who we were, to the one block area with four crossing side streets and bundles, piles and boxes of everything. The watch was not a new pristine Patel, or anything valuable. He was seething. I held his arm as we scoured every corner. We finally saw it, looked up at the crook who said 30 dollars. Lance wound up to flatten him. My purse was yanked out from under my arm. A knife cut the strap. I shouted, Lance! He hadn't landed the blow, grabbed my assailant, his head toward me, and I knocked him to stumbles. I took my purse and the knife. There were too many angry eyes around us. We beat it out of there post haste.

Lance was still steaming as we went into the hotel lobby and sat. The manager came over seeing the anger that was bubbling over. I stopped him and asked him to come back after we had a drink. One drink for Lance would never solve an issue like this. I comforted him with every feminine wile that can be applied in public.

Eventually, he settled and the manager returned. The conversation settled to 'civil". The guy apologized over and over for what he had no control. He continued with his troubles which were dovetailed right back into thievery. Inadvertently he painted a damning picture of what life in this city was like.

We went back up to the room, I poured him a triple and put us au natural under a sheet which we didn't need at the Equator. This was for him and I didn't let him go until he was too tired to please. Secretly I was disappointed that as a Seal I hadn't handled that situation with more broken bones and faces.

We awoke together and I asked him if he needed more stress medicine. Happily, for me, the devil was back in his eye and everyone overdosed.

We limited ourselves to the hotel restaurant, avoiding the jostling bar. An old guy who had seen our "hurting" the night before slid over next to our bar stools. Native English speaker, his frame, sophistication, and presence led Lance to ask if he was

British and/or, had been a diver. We divers can smell each other out.

"Yes, I have been, and have been around the world. I haven't been to Rab. People say it's mostly good for wreck dives. I like healthy, lovely reefs with an abundance of fish. Unfortunately, I settled here and have dived only twice in ten years."

Both our ears pricked up at that. Vanna, soothingly asked why that was.

"Alfonse was his name, "Alfi". He continued, "I had no idea when I came here how unbelievable an underwater habitat could be."

Lance gently prodded, "And?"

"Ever hear of El Nino?"

Lance carefully, "Of course. Does it come near shore here?"

Alfi guffawed, "It comes all the f…king way up the beach here. It's an underwater steam roller. Mind you, it doesn't come every year. Sometimes once a year sometimes two, sometimes remnants even three."

Lance isn't coy anymore, "What problems does it cause? Flooding, landslides, washouts? How would that affect diving?"

"Lance, my boy, if I may, flooding, landslides, or washouts, from my point of view are minor. The damage is not directly on land, it is a destroyer of the bottom and the reef. It rampages over reefs leaving brush. It doesn't come for two or three years. Thin traces begin to grow, some fish re-appear, and wham, year three. Only crusty rock bottoms."

It takes thousands of years to grow a reef. It is so unpredictable that few divers risk their monies on what may not only be sparse, but completely razed by the time they get here. Your ideas of parasailing also suffer. Scuba and parasailing have an interconnected existence. One enhances the other. You will see only three parasailing businesses within forty miles north and south of the city.

CHAPTER TWENTY-ONE

Fallback

Alfi wasn't drunk. We waited another day and went carefully down to the seafood restaurants whose pilings were deep in the structure of the beach. No jewelry, watches, or purses in view. Bouncers, no crooks. Money only on me in places Lance finds interesting. Watching for other people with diverse appearances; sipping a few aqua-vits. The experiences that confirm Alfi's sad story came sometimes with wet eyes.

CHAPTER TWENTY-TWO

Back-Up, Thank Goodness

Until we had several drinks on the three flights, plane changes and layovers, we were quiet.

With a deep sigh, Lance comes conscious, "Lucky we did our homework with fallbacks. The pick-pockets were enough in themselves to drive me out. What a secret El Nino has hidden.

Vanna agrees, "If I lived there for six months, I would probably kill three thieves per month. Our backup on Rab is pleasant with friends and growing ties. Greg and Cheryl, a nice bonus. Neither of us is so decimated that we can't teach scuba from the pier and with an assistant, run a full parasailing adventure.

CHAPTER TWENTY-THREE

A Dragon Lives Forever, Not So Little Boys

The ideas studied before the uncomfortable journey to Guayaquil included options. There was a small bay just a few hundred meters from the resort dock we had used for years. Some structures had been renovated into homes. Three of the five structures were near the surf. Two that could be houses were abandoned. The third was right on the beach and could serve as a warehouse for tanks and parasail equipment, including the now-arrived security boat from Guanaja. The other three structures were higher up the side hill, maybe fifty feet. They were twins in construction. The third was fifty feet higher set above and between the twins. A few yards above the upper house were a tramway that had in its time provided a pathway for every can of paint, plank, or bag of groceries. It had remained serviceable and without that cable car, living in the upper house, our choice would have been untenable.

We chose that and carved out the working relationship with the two boys, now men, handling Bearn's original scuba resort, which we had owned until anticipated retirement. In the transfer, we stipulated twenty percent of yearly profits. Money was not an issue. We had hundreds of thousands from the sale of the Guanaja property to Roberto. We still received a check bi-annually for ten percent of the net profits there.

We also agreed that we, to keep busy, would run, in our bay, a beginner scuba class. Members who met safety standards would be seconded back to Bearn's for advanced training. We also kept the security boat for parasailing. A useful partnership blossomed.

CHAPTER TWENTY-FOUR

Realities

Marko and Petra gave forth a little boy for whom we shouldered the pleasure of grandparents, once removed. Petra had healed and was able to dive again so we saw her frequently with little Petar pegged to her thighs. She made an exerted effort to bring us close to her family, especially Petar, whom she hoped to leave with us as babysitters while she dived, sometimes for a day or two.

Peter started with us before he was able to swim and by age 12 was fully trained in scuba. We also sweetened the deal by taking him parasailing. We spent many days and open-fire nights with him while Petra was gone and Marko working. We took him up to Munich to meet Greg and Cheryl. He was old enough to enjoy the folk-dance show in the Hofbrau house.

He would come from school every day, even raining, and spend time with us before going home to do homework. He worked on every element of the resort that didn't need a professional tech. He went over to Bearn's resort for advanced training. He cajoled his mother to take him to where he could see some real reef. We went along.

He helped us with renovation on the upper house noting the increase in invasion of the surf into the bay. We were glad we chose the upper house with global warming in mind.

Eventually, Petra and Marko decided to send him to 11th and 12th grade boarding school. Marko remembered his challenges in moving into a dorm in a U.S. university. He thought boarding school would allay that.

Vanna and I were only honorary grandparents so kept to ourselves. We knew what a huge hole that would put in our lives. The boarding school regimen started and he called us occasionally on zoom. We conversed back and for with Petra and Marko keeping everyone parent-wise in the loop.

When the first two-week break started, he spent the first night with his parents and most of the entire time with us in the anti-surf rooms. Immersed in the water borne life with scuba and parasailing he was enthralled. The break ended, and for the first time the good-bye was punctuated with deep hugs.

Vanna and Lance lived on keeping each other very warm in and around the bedroom. They ventured into the town and met a few friends that 'stuck'. Some cards. Some chess, Uber for beers. A few visited them in the above surf house. As time went by, expectedly Petar would visit or contact them less and less.

CHAPTER TWENTY-FIVE

Sensing The Impending Too Late.

Looking at the strength of the surf on a daily basis showed little change. Comparing after a year, and then two, something appeared to be concerned about. The one country doing the greedy-most to carbon gas the atmosphere was the U.S. led still by Republicans profiting from the lobbyists from the fossil fuel industry and interfering with monies for investments in renewable energy. Sick! We voted absentee but couldn't "donate" enough money to buy congressmen. We would suffer the destruction.

CHAPTER TWENTY-SIX

Anticipated Impacts

One day at sundown, we looked out at the waves in the bay and continued down the tram to the house. Not aware of what was happening with the surf, we were surprised when we got a dousing of salt water. We scurried up to the top floor and the wash no longer pelted. Worried about what could happen if we went out and tried to send up the tram, we stayed. Rogue waves more than fifty feet high crashing every object in their way. We hugged and heard the generator come on right next to us at the top vent outside. Waterproof lighting on the dock came on giving a hurried look at the wild water. Watching carefully and defensively, we saw the waning intensity. Surf receded, not to where it had been. We found a trunk of dry blankets and fitfully slept the rest of the night in the attic. One floor down sleep would be inundated.

At daybreak, they looked out and saw the mess. They started re-organizing the interior and .... in charge Petar. He headed to them for once-forgotten hugs.

He huffed, "I thought you might be swept away or under the water, or something. What do you need? I can arrange to return to class a few days later considering the circumstances."

Lance answers, "You can begin by helping Vanna. I need to talk to your parents about the protocol for missing school. Cell phone towers are inland enough to be functioning. I should be able to get them. I doubt the wave would have affected them that far inland. You know that and slept there last night, didn't you?"

"Gramps, I didn't. My bus was delayed and all I heard on the radio placed you directly in the wall of water. My knapsack is upstairs outside the door." Lance, "OK, you can stay for a while. I want your folks to know you are all right."

"Petra, he is with us. His bus was late and he heard the news and guessed correctly that we were in the middle of the destruction. His help would be critical considering the damage here. God, I forgot Bearn's marina. I've got to get over there right now. I need to take Petar and Vanna with me and we'll plan accordingly later. Sorry to be so short! Bye."

Lance, "Come on you two, up the tram. The pick-up is there and will be faster. Watch carefully and tell me of any possible rescues needed from us or danger to us."

CHAPTER TWENTY-SEVEN

Neighbors Together

The two men and apprentice were on their feet outside the house, glory be. They provided us some coffee and we quickly tried to set some priorities for the two properties. Their main residence was significantly further from the surf line than ours. We would have to concentrate quickly on the boat supply house, the sports equipment, the dock, and boats now lapping ten meters from the dock. With six of us, we quickly put those things back together. They would have to look at their house soon. The late Anika's house was built well above the water line at the time of planning and no rooms were flooded. It was becoming very clear about the judgment and territorial knowledge of Bearn and the sea. I asked them to come help at our house until the heavy lifting was done.

CHAPTER TWENTY-EIGHT

The Evil Lobby Grinds On,
More Will Come

The contribution of the Republicans and their well-healed lobbyists floated on. Other countries with little foresight damaged the earth daily. The surf which had been moving up the beach under the dock was now hitting the sand shore a foot higher. It never returned to its previous levels.

The scuba training began again and parasailing increased by fits and starts. We moved back into the upper house. There were some high surfs occasionally doing no damage. Then reality hit!

The higher surfs made no impact on the main wreck-diving resort. It was located hundreds of yards down outside the bay. The shape of the bay shoveled huge washes of surf into a deluge into Lance and Vanna's operation squeezing and gaining deadly force. They jockeyed equipment around to stay safe. They were not contentedly in town playing when the next rogue hit, and hard. As they ran up to their front porch, angry water lapped at their ankles. It rose like a snake and pulled any loose materials down to break on the rocks. Lance grabbed an axe and her arm. They scrambled upstairs to the main living floor. Hoping this would be the extent of the disaster, they stopped in the living room to catch their breaths. The water surged up the stairs and around the stairwell forcing them up into the attic. Water reached their ankles again.

Lance growled, "I am not going to spend a lifetime in the sea to drown in a dam attic." Sinewy shoulders threw the axe hard into the roof. Water continued to rise. Getting the purchase of the axe out of the water caused him to slip and lose balance. Vanna was there holding him and suddenly shrieked, "Lance, stop. It's reached its peak here. Watch, its draining."

It was up to their waists and Lance was making little headway into the tarred roof. He stopped and they both stared heartbeats thumping.

In baseball, three strikes and you're out. They had had their two strikes. Friends and scuba leaders hauled their belongings into the house that Bearn built.

CHAPTER TWENTY-NINE

A PIVOT: Thanks, Ron J. We're out of our careers and you want to defund Social Security

Lance and I now lived full-time in Anika's indestructible house. Our operation in the bay was closed and what remained of the houses was fenced off from unwary wanderers. The frequency and thunder of water coming into the nature-made gorge couldn't be nailed down. We awkwardly attempted to help the boys, now men in the Starr2 resort.

Lance holds Vanna in the thick German Bedcover and they enter their post-loving bubble.

"Honey, I'm sure you agree we are spinning our wheels here. I'm getting embarrassed that we are living in what really belongs to the resort. We're getting our percentage but are interfering with whatever expansion they might be hoping to build. I have some ideas of how we might be able to support the resort, not from here. Let's go up to Munich and see what Cheryl and Greg might advise."

We tucked ourselves in with them for a week and hammered out a clean new career for us. Beer and wine for stimulating the right brain, getting sober completed intense pros and cons of the left. Cheryl was excited to live closer to us near the Hirshgarten. Gruffly Greg signed onto the idea which was important for Lance, now friends and partners in Mercedes for decades. The usual parting shot from his reverie: "We don't want too much noise around here" drew our warm smile. He shuddered back into his lost world of untested inventions."

CHAPTER THIRTY

Career-Topping Waning Years

I guided Vanna to Marienstrasse, remembering the experience with the undressed model years before my old friend. Before I met Vanna, the model did entice marketing for Guanaja. I wisely held the memory and spoke with the realtor selecting a shop with a window on the major thoroughfare. It was the ideal location and our finances covered it easily. We named it LaVanna Packaged Gear, Inc. featuring gear and snorkeling of the Croatian Coast. We got out of underfoot of the diving camp with the purchase of an antique German-style house across from an entrance to the Hirsch-Garten.

CHAPTER THIRTY-ONE

A New Career Start

A somewhat more liberal group around Marienstrasse thought it quite cute to have a couple of Americans interested in planting a new business in such a competitive area. Upon further review of what the business was, they wondered more.

The environment began with quality decorators guided by Vanna. We hired a model to double her eye candy. With some pieces of scuba wear, she showed a fanciful idea of what the purchaser might look like. Plaster models are sometimes substituted for gorgeous live women with not much more than scuba gear attached. Presentation racks followed the undersea colors of wetsuit wear. Changing rooms and utilities in the back with large boxes of a variety of sizes and shapes, usually requested by well-endowed women. A large aquarium with underwater creatures brought from the reef south of the Starr resort caught all passers-by's imagination. It was a splendid, sophisticated atmosphere. The neighbors couldn't fault that. The marketing study pointed toward sophisticated clientele and the highest quality name-brand merchandise.

The sales bloomed when we advertised a 'custom-made' diving dress and adaptable under-sea equipment. Dress and equipment. Found to market research, there were no similar sales and services in any nearby area. The key service was the custom-made trade. Marketing research had not overlooked the 'size' of the population. We could re-size for small people if they came our way. Mainly, those who came our way, sometimes shyly, needed sizing very much the opposite. Their nature was not of the middle class. They would pay handsomely for dresses that enhanced their positive attributes and reduced the noticeability of the negative.

Both Vanna and I had dealt with that desire mostly with clients who came on scuba resort stays.

At first contact, Vanna stepped forward. She had more languages with more fluency than I, not to mention poise and femininity. Comfort came to our major customer, the tens of clients who were women. They saw Vanna or our living model and decided what they were, she could do for them. Vanna became immediately a confidant as well, skilled in sizing whatever bulge or valley that needed hiding. Some might consider Vanna's shape and charm a form of false advertising. These were wealthy people who would consider any notable improvement a confidence-raising attraction. All had fallen prey to German food and drink. Stylish enlargement of wetsuit stock was immediately used and large sizes were put on order. There were more bumps and valleys to develop.

Suddenly the shop was a draw for large numbers of wealthy women who shopped on whims in entrenched nearby liberal businesses. Originally, owners had been distantly welcoming; and had had doubts about our chance of success. We had hit a niche!

Vanna smiles, "There was no doubt now and we were welcomed across the street in Gasthaus Pferd Und Flanke where new customers, good draft, and friends were frequent. Lance became the jolly, interesting American with adventures to share."

We visited the Starr2 less frequently as the years went by. With Lance's German notably fluent, we had social lives that bloomed. We learned much about the city and traveled to taste different brews in scores of different dorfs.

Slowly we began to inhabit more the Pferd, and chapters of our life escaped to friends over the bar. All around were friends and immediately I saw an opportunity for many nights of entertainment by their adopted Americans. I drank Lager and Vanna Weisbeer. We were welcomed to the Stamtisch and another chapter was born. Our eyes met and of like mind, we made our excuses and caught a taxi back to the Hirsch-garten.

With new friends and excitement sparking them, the thick German comforters spent most of the time on the floor. Intense loving was still alive.

Vanna was beginning to move into the pretzel from the bubble when Lance whispered, "Vanna, this was a spectacular night for me. I need to enter myself into the bar scene with some caution. Going there every night or even every other night I think is too much. Obviously, you know the many stories I can recount or enhance. You know them because they are us. I want you there or I won't go. Perhaps we could start with a limit of three nights per week."

Vanna smiles a Jim Neighbor's smile and responds. "Lance, this is sincerely not corny. When I see you having such a good time, and at the same time hear the trials and secrets of our life together, my heart fills with joy."

"Ok, we'll try Tuesday, Friday, and Saturday starting not before seven p.m. ending promptly at ten. After that hour, I have other pressing business." His eyes now the devil, anticipate carefully the flash in Vanna's.

Their routine worked out in many ways. Keeping to it kept them physically and emotionally grounded. In a few years with some repeated stories they became an attraction in their burrow. Beer became free. They moderated it. Love only bloomed, never aged.

One Tuesday, neither of them came. No-one knew what to think and just waited hopefully for Friday. On Friday, only Lance appeared. He maintained his joviality at his best. Didn't drink any beer. On Friday he came alone again. Those who knew him for years noticed the difference in his eyes. He drank no beer and only made it through two short stories. One was the intimacy of the dive after Vanna's first kiss under his wetsuit. The other the explosion of her jealousy over Zulinda's non-clothing arrival at the planning of a response to cartel encroachment of Roberto's shrimp business.

CHAPTER THIRTY-TWO

Bearn's Prophesy

On Saturday he came no more. There were pictures of him and Vanna in the office behind the bar. Some made efforts to locate them or him. No sign whatsoever. Ulrich, the gasthof owner lost good friends and the GUMEIKLIKEIT they enthused..

Bear's Prophesy Realized:

After the initial screening for Starr2, Bearn and Anika sat closely behind the curtain at their kitchen table. They watched the two newly tested owners of Starr2 resort look slyly around and share a kiss worthy of merit. Looking carefully again, they walked bonded like matching puzzle pieces up the misty hill melding into one person.

Bearn's eyes glossed over long enough for Anika to note. He returned from his reverie, not smiling. Anika knew his looks after 45 years. This was new territory. "Bearn, what? This is not you. Why?"

He took her hand tightly.

"Those two people are in an emotional bond of incomparable strength. The frivolity we see is far thinner than what is lurking below. Whatever their future may bring, within six weeks of the passing of one, the other will disappear never to be found."

Anika snickers, "Oh Bearn, you old brute, with me you already have too many witches."

Bearn's prophecy did not die with him.

Eventually on a Saturday, you would enter the Pferd through the main entrance and on the wall above the end of the bar, a picture. It was embossed and framed. It said:

"In life, a man as caring as Lance Starr could find no richer prize than Vanna Richards to share a protective, enduring adventure. TOGETHER, THEY WERE AS ONE."

--Roberto F.

Owner, Starr Resort1
Guanaja, Bay Islands

End of Book Three, Guanaja Defense, The Last Resort